Pirate Attack!

By Deborah Lock

Senior Editor Caryn Jenner
Editor Nandini Gupta
Art Editors Emma Hobson, Shruti Soharia Singh
Jacket Editor Francesca Young
Jacket Designers Amy Keast
DTP Designer Anita Yadav
Picture Researcher Aditya Katyal
Producer, Pre-Production Nadine King
Producer Niamh Tierney
Managing Editor Laura Gilbert
Deputy Managing Editor Vineetha Mokkil
Managing Art Editors Diane Peyton Jones
Art Director Martin Wilson
Publisher Sarah Larter
Publishing Director Sophie Mitchell

Educational consultant
Jacqueline Harris

First published in Great Britain in 2017
by Dorling Kindersley Limited
80 Strand, London, WC2R 0RL

A CIP catalogue record for this book is available from the British Library.

ISBN: 978-0-2413-0584-3

Printed and bound in China.

The publisher would like to thank the following for their kind permission to reproduce their photographs:
(Key: a-above; b-below/bottom; c-centre; f-far; l-left; r-right; t-top)

All other images © Dorling Kindersley
For further information see: www.dkimages.com

A WORLD OF IDEAS:
SEE ALL THERE IS TO KNOW

www.dk.com

Contents

Words in **bold** appear in the glossary.

Get Ready to Sail

Pirates sailed the seas. They took **treasure** from other ships. Their favourite kind of treasure was gold.

"Ahoy, matey!"

That's how pirates said hello.

Ahoy! I'll tell you all about pirates.

Pirate Ship

mast

sail

rudder

hull

These are the
main parts of a ship.

rigging

main deck

Chapter 1

Setting Sail

A pirate ship needed a captain and **crew**. The captain was in charge. The crew had different jobs. Sometimes, children worked in pirate crews. They even got a small share of the treasure.

One of the most famous pirates was Blackbeard. People were scared to fight with Blackbeard. That made it easier for him to steal their treasure.

Blackbeard had many pirate ships. His biggest ship was called *Queen Anne's Revenge*.

Wanted Dead or Alive!

Blackbeard

Real name: **Edward Teach**

(Beware! He is very dangerous.)

"Hoist the sails" means to put them up so the wind can blow the ship along.

When it was time to set sail, the pirate captain gave the orders.

"Lift the **anchor**!"

"Hoist the sails!"

The crew pulled up the anchor and raised the sails. Then the ship sailed out to sea!

Pirate Rules

Here are some rules that pirate crews had to follow.

 Obey the captain.

 No fighting on board the ship.

 Keep **weapons** clean and ready for battle.

 Lights out at 8 o'clock at night.

PIRATES WHO BROKE THE RULES WERE PUNISHED!

These were some punishments.

 Painful lashes with a whip.

Help!

Ouch!

 Being left alone on an island.

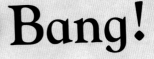

Bang!

 Being shot with a pistol.

Chapter 2
Life on Board

Do you think pirate ships were comfortable?

Life could be hard on board a pirate ship. Pirates were at sea for a long time. They often slept in hammocks below **deck**. There were plenty of rats below deck, too.

Pirates couldn't be fussy about their food!

Pirates had to eat whatever the ship's cook prepared. Fresh food started to rot after a while. Then the pirates ate food that had been dried or covered with salt. This made the food last longer.

Pirate Food

Pirates often spent months
at sea, so they needed food
that would last.

salt

sacks of
grain

salted meat

Limes and other citrus
fruits kept pirates healthy,
but soon rotted.

citrus fruit

barrels
of food

dried fruit

There was a lot of work to do on a pirate ship. The crew made sure the ship was in good repair so it didn't sink. They scrubbed the decks and kept the ship clean.

Pirates also had fun. They played musical instruments and sang songs called **sea shanties**. They often sang sea shanties while they worked.

Pirate Sea Shanty

Pretend you're on a pirate ship
and sing this sea shanty!

A pirate's life is the life for me.
Yo ho ho and a bottle of rum!
On a ship so fine we'll sail out
to sea.
Yo ho ho and a bottle of rum!

Here with my hearties, we'll
travel the waves,
And those who cross us end
up in their graves.

We fight to the last.
We are brave and so bold,
And share out the treasure
of glittering gold.

So sing loud the tune and
bang on the drum.
Yo ho ho and a bottle of rum!

In this sea shanty,
which words rhyme
with rum and gold?

What was the treasure?

What is a heartie?

Chapter 3

Battle at Sea

Pirates climbed up to the top of the ship to look out to sea. They could see a long way from up there!

If a pirate spotted another ship, he called out, "Sail ho!"

That was the signal. The pirate captain would order his crew to get their weapons ready.

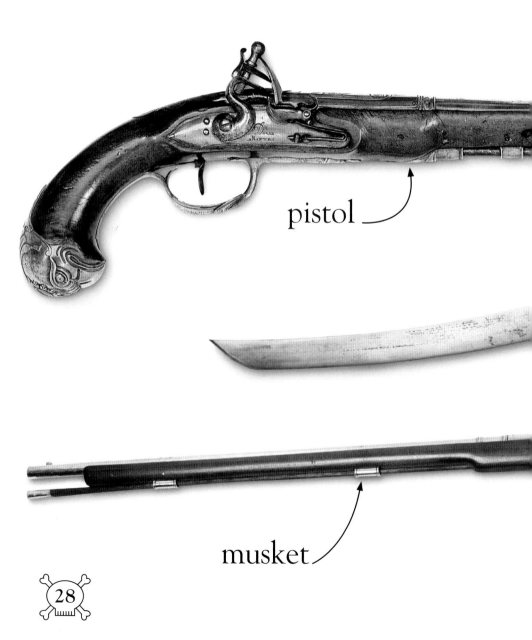

pistol

musket

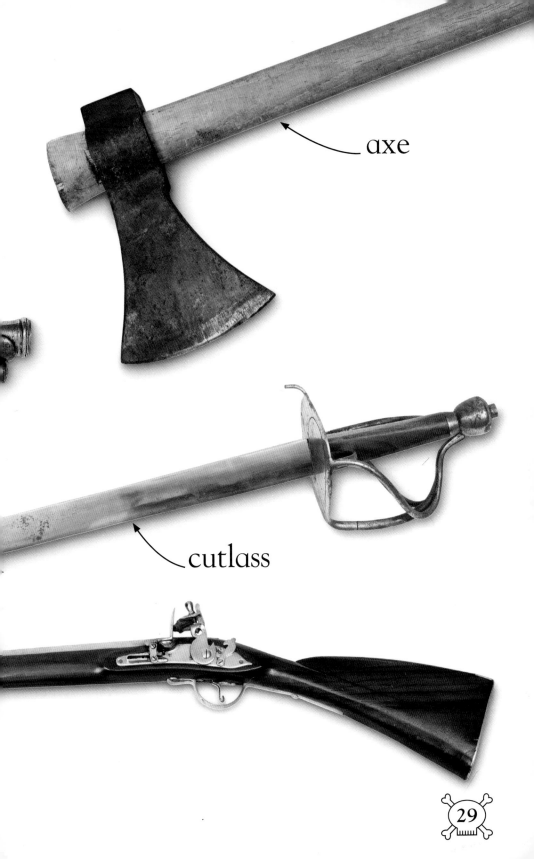

axe

cutlass

Pirate ships flew a black flag called a Jolly Roger. The Jolly Roger warned other ships that pirates were coming!

The pirates hoped that the crew of the other ship might give up. That way the pirates could take their treasure without a fight.

If the other crew didn't give up, then the pirates attacked. First they fired the cannon.

Bang!

Then the pirates fought with the crew of the other ship. They didn't stop fighting until they got what they wanted – treasure!

Treasure

Most ships carried **cargo** such as sugar and spices. Pirates could sell these things for money. Of course, the best kind of treasure was gold!

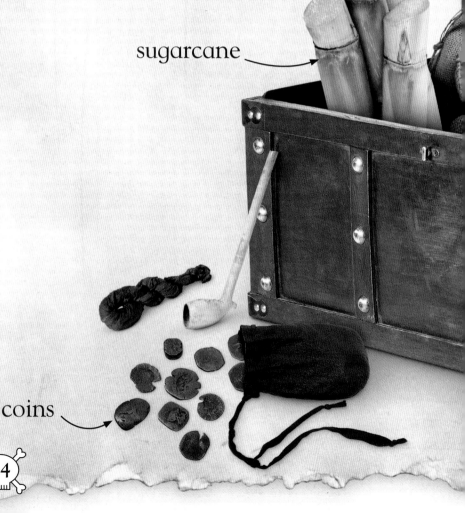

sugarcane

coins

spices

Chapter 4

Land Ahoy!

After a battle, the pirates sailed on. Sometimes, they searched for another ship to rob.

Sometimes, they sailed towards land. They might want to find a place to spend their treasure!

On land, the pirates could have a rest from sailing. They could repair their ship, and buy food and supplies. They could spend their treasure, too!

Land ahoy!

Some pirates sailed to deserted islands. No one lived on these islands. Many people think that pirates buried their treasure on deserted islands.

The idea of buried treasure probably came from books such as **Treasure Island**, by Robert Louis Stevenson.

However, most pirates didn't really bury their treasure. They spent it or traded it for other things. Pirates were too greedy!

Pirate Lingo

Pirates had their own way of speaking. Here are some pirate words.

Yo ho ho!
(Say when happy)

Ahoy, mateys!
(Hello, friends!)

Ahoy! Did you know that most real pirates did not have pet parrots?

Seadog
(An old pirate)

Heave ho!
(Push)

Pieces of eight
(Coins)

Shiver me timbers!
(Say when shocked)

Booty!
(Treasure)

Pirate Quiz

1. How did pirates say "hello"?

2. What was Blackbeard's real name?

3. What does "hoist the sails" mean?

4. What did pirates sleep in?

5. What was the Jolly Roger?

 Answers on page 48.

Glossary

anchor something heavy used to stop the ship from moving

cargo things taken from one place to another on a ship

crew people working on a ship

deck floor of a ship

sea shanties songs sung by sailors

treasure things that are worth a lot of money

Treasure Island famous book about pirates written in 1883

weapons tools for fighting

Guide for Parents

DK Readers is an exciting four-level reading series for children that will help to develop the habit of reading widely for both pleasure and information. These chapter books have an engaging main narrative to suit your child's reading ability, interspersed with additional information spreads in a range of reading genres. Each book is designed to develop your child's reading skills, fluency, grammar awareness, and comprehension in order to build confidence and pleasure in reading.

Ready for a *Beginning to Read* book

YOUR CHILD SHOULD

- be using phonics, including consonant blends, such as br, sp and st, to sound out unfamiliar words; and be familiar with common word endings, such as plurals, ing, ed, and ly.
- be using the meaning of the text, the grammar of a sentence, plus clues from the illustrations to check and correct his/her own reading.
- be pausing briefly at commas, and for longer at full stops; and altering his/her expression for question, exclamation, and speech marks.

A VALUABLE AND SHARED READING EXPERIENCE

For many children, reading requires a lot of effort, but adult participation can make this both fun and easier. So here are a few tips on how to use this book with your child.

TIP 1 Check out the contents together before your child begins:
- read the text about the book on the back cover.
- read through and discuss the contents page together to heighten your child's interest and expectation.
- have a brief discussion about unfamiliar or difficult words on each page.
- chat about the non-fiction reading features used in the book, such as headings, captions, and labels.

TIP 2 Support your child as he/she reads each page:

- give the book to your child to read and turn the pages.
- where necessary, encourage your child to break a word into syllables, sound out each one, and then flow the syllables together. Ask him/her to reread the sentence to check the meaning.
- you may need to help read some topic-related vocabulary and other words that may be difficult for your child.
- when there's a question mark or an exclamation mark, encourage your child to vary his/her voice as he/she reads the sentence. Demonstrate how to do this if it is helpful.

TIP 3 Praise, share and chat:

- the additional information spreads are designed to be shared and discussed with your child. These spreads tend to be more difficult than the main narrative.
- ask your child questions about the meaning of the text and of the words used. This will help to develop comprehension skills and awareness of the language used.

A FEW ADDITIONAL TIPS

- Encourage your child to try reading difficult words by themselves. Praise any self-corrections, for example, "I like the way you sounded out that word and then changed the way you said it to make sense."
- Try to read together every day. Reading little and often is best. These books are divided into manageable chapters for one reading session. However, after 10 minutes, only keep going if your child wants to read on.
- Read a variety of books of different types with your child for pleasure and information. Reading aloud to your child is a great way to develop his or her reading skills!
- Make reading an enjoyable experience for your child.

Index

Answers to the Pirate Quiz:
1. Ahoy, matey!; 2. Edward Teach; 3. Put up the sails; 4. Hammock; 5. Pirates' flag.